W9-AKW-614

ERIC CARLE

A House for Hermit Crab

Newt☀n
EDUCATION FOUNDATION
Creating A Culture of Support for Education.

Scan the QR code to hear the story read to you.

READY-TO-READ

SIMON SPOTLIGHT

New York   London   Toronto   Sydney   New Delhi

This book was previously published with slightly different text.

For my son Rolf

SIMON SPOTLIGHT
An imprint of Simon & Schuster Children's Publishing Division
1230 Avenue of the Americas, New York, New York 10020
Copyright © 1987 Eric Carle Corporation
Eric Carle's name and signature logo type are registered trademarks of Eric Carle.
First Simon Spotlight Ready-to-Read edition 2014
All rights reserved, including the right of reproduction in whole or in part in any form.
SIMON SPOTLIGHT, READY-TO-READ, and colophon are registered trademarks of Simon & Schuster, Inc.
For information about special discounts for bulk purchases, please contact Simon & Schuster Special Sales at
1-866-506-1949 or business@simonandschuster.com.
The Simon & Schuster Speakers Bureau can bring authors to your live event. For more information or to book an event
contact the Simon & Schuster Speakers Bureau at 1-866-248-3049 or visit our website at www.simonspeakers.com.
Manufactured in the United States of America 0221 LAK
10 9 8
Library of Congress Cataloging-in-Publication Data
Carle, Eric.
A house for Hermit Crab / Eric Carle. — First edition.
pages cm. — (Ready-to-read. Level 2)
"First Simon Spotlight Ready-to-Read edition."
Originally published in a slightly different form by Picture Book Studio in Saxonville,
Massachusetts, 1987.
Summary: A hermit crab who has outgrown his old shell moves into a new one, which
he decorates and enhances with the various sea creatures he meets in his travels.
[1. Hermit crabs—Fiction. 2. Crabs—Fiction. 3. Marine animals—Fiction. 4. Dwellings—Fiction.] 1. Title.
PZ7.C21476Hp 2014
[E]—dc23
2013030571
ISBN 978-1-4814-0915-5 (pbk)
ISBN 978-1-4814-0916-2 (hc)

This book was previously published with slightly different text.

"It's time to move," said Hermit Crab
one day in January. "I've grown
too big for this little shell."

Hermit Crab had felt safe and snug
in his shell. But now it was too snug.
He stepped out of the shell
and onto the floor of the ocean.
But it was frightening out in the
open sea without a shell to hide in.

"What if a big fish comes along and attacks me?" he thought. "I must find a new house soon."

Early in February, Hermit Crab found
just the house he was looking for.
It was a big shell, and strong. He moved
right in, wiggling and waggling about
inside it to see how it felt. It felt just right.

"But it looks so—well, so *plain*," thought Hermit Crab.

In March, Hermit Crab met some sea anemones. They swayed gently back and forth in the water.

"How beautiful you are!"
said Hermit Crab. "Would one of you
be willing to come and live on my
house? It is so plain, it needs you."

"I'll come," whispered a small
sea anemone.

Gently, Hermit Crab picked it up
with his claw and put it on his shell.

In April, Hermit Crab passed
a flock of starfish moving slowly
along the sea floor.

"How handsome you are!"
said Hermit Crab. "Would one of you
be willing to decorate my house?"

"I would," signaled a little sea star.
Hermit Crab picked it up
with his claw and put it on his house.

In May, Hermit Crab discovered
some coral. They were hard,
and didn't move.
"How pretty you are!"
said Hermit Crab. "Would one of you
be willing to help make my house
more beautiful?

"I would," creaked a crusty coral. Carefully, Hermit Crab picked it up with his claw and placed it on his shell.

In June, Hermit Crab came upon
a group of snails crawling over a rock
on the ocean floor. They grazed
as they went, picking up algae
and bits of debris, and leaving
a neat path behind them.

"How tidy and hard-working you are!"
said Hermit Crab. "Would one of you
be willing to help clean my house?"

"I would," offered one of the snails.

Happily, Hermit Crab picked it up
with his claw and placed it on his shell.

In July, Hermit Crab came upon
several sea urchins. They had sharp,
prickly needles.
"How fierce you look!"
said Hermit Crab. "Would one of you
be willing to protect my house?"

"I would," answered a spiky sea urchin.
Gratefully, Hermit Crab picked it up
with his claw and placed it
near his shell.

In August, Hermit Crab and his friends
wandered into a forest of seaweed.

"It's so dark here,"
thought Hermit Crab.
"How dim it is,"
murmured the sea anemone.
"How gloomy it is,"
whispered the starfish.
"How murky it is,"
complained the coral.
"I can't see!" said the snail.
"It's like nighttime!"
cried the sea urchin.

In September, Hermit Crab spotted
a school of lanternfish
darting through the dark water.
"How bright you are!" said Hermit Crab.
"Would one of you be willing
to light up our house?"

"I would," replied one lanternfish.
And it swam over near the shell.

In October, Hermit Crab
approached a pile of smooth pebbles.
"How sturdy you are!"
said Hermit Crab. "Would you mind
if I rearranged you?"

"Not at all," answered the pebbles.
Hermit Crab picked them up
one by one with his claw
and built a wall around his shell.
"Now my house is perfect!"
cheered Hermit Crab.

But in November, Hermit Crab
felt that his shell was a bit too small.
Little by little, over the year,
Hermit Crab had grown. Soon
he would have to find another,
bigger home.

But he had come to love his friends,
the sea anemone, the starfish,
the coral, the sea urchin, the snail,
the lanternfish, and even
the smooth pebbles.

"They have been so good to me,"
thought Hermit Crab. "They are like
a family. How can I ever leave them?"

In December, a smaller
hermit crab passed by.
"I have outgrown my shell," she said.
"Would you know of a place for me?"

"I have outgrown *my* house too,"
answered Hermit Crab. "I must
move on. You are welcome
to live here—but you must promise
to be good to my friends."

"I promise," said the little crab.

The following January, Hermit Crab stepped out and the little crab moved in.

"I couldn't stay in that little shell forever," said Hermit Crab as he waved goodbye.